BLIMPING
BUFFALO

First published in 2010 by Hodder Children's Books
This paperback edition published in 2011

Text copyright © Bruce Hobson 2010
Illustrations copyright © Adrienne Kennaway 2010

Hodder Children's Books, 338 Euston Road, London, NW1 3BH

Hodder Children's Books Australia
Level 17/207 Kent Street, Sydney, NSW 2000

A catalogue record of this book is available from the British Library.

ISBN: 978 0 340 98936 4

Printed in China

Hodder Children's Books is a division of Hachette Children's Books.
An Hachette UK Company.
www.hachette.co.uk

BUMPING BUFFALO

Written by
Mwenye Hadithi

Illustrated by
Adrienne Kennaway

h
Hodder
Children's
Books

A division of Hachette Children's Books

Bumping Buffalo liked to bump. He had great big horns with a huge pad in the middle, just right for bumping.

Buffalo would bump
anything and everything;
he bumped animals,
he bumped trees,
and some days he even
bumped rocks.

When the other buffaloes were happily chewing grass together, Bumping Buffalo was out on his own looking for things to bump.

BUMP!

He bumped Rhino who was nibbling the tasty leaves of a Toothbrush Bush.

Rhino shouted, "Go away! Are you looking for trouble?"

He bumped Elephant who was leaning against
a Pepper-bark Tree having a snooze.

BUMP!
BUMP!

Elephant shouted, "Stop doing that! Are you looking for trouble?"

Buffalo just laughed.

Then he bumped a Baobab Tree very hard.

BUMP! BUMP! BUMP!

Bush-baby was sleeping in the top of the tree.
She fell off her branch and came bouncing
down through the leaves.

"One day all this bumping will get you into trouble, and then you'll be sorry!" she complained sleepily.

Buffalo went off to find other things to bump.

It began to rain and Bumping Buffalo took shelter under an Umbrella Tree next to a large cave in the rocks. Big Zebra and Small Zebra came by.

He was about to bump them when he heard Big Zebra say, "You must never go near that cave. There is nothing but trouble in there."

When Big Zebra saw Buffalo she added loudly, "Of course, if you ARE looking for trouble, that is where you will find it."

Buffalo jumped up. He had been looking for trouble for so long and at last he had found it!

He was sure it was going to be fun to bump. Buffalo puffed himself up, shook his huge horns, kicked up clouds of dust with his hooves, and charged into the cave, bellowing fiercely.

It was pitch black in the cave.
He slid to a halt and looked around.
At first he couldn't see anything.

When he could see a little more, he saw a pair of eyes.
He tried to bump them with his horns, but he couldn't.

Then he saw another pair of eyes, and another,
and another and another, and he heard a loud

GROWWWLING!

Suddenly Buffalo felt himself being
bitten by lots of very sharp
teeth. They pinched his hooves,
they nipped his ankles, they
bit his legs and they
chomped on his knees.

Then they gnawed at
his tail. Then they
chewed his nose. And it

HURT!

Bumping Buffalo bumped and bumped, but it was
no use. He turned and ran out of the cave,
chased by a pack of angry howling Wild Dogs.
He ran and he ran and he ran.

"Ah! So you found trouble at last," said Rhino,
as Buffalo panted past the Toothbrush Bush.

The Wild Dogs chased
him and chased him,
and he ran even further.

"Ah! So you found
trouble at last," said Elephant,
as Buffalo hurtled past
the Pepper-bark Tree.

When he was quite lost and exhausted, Bumping Buffalo hid behind a large Baobab Tree where the Wild Dogs could not find him. Then he bumped the tree, just for fun.

"Stop doing that!" yelled Bush-baby
sleepily from the high branches.
So the Wild Dogs saw Buffalo and
they chased him and chased
him all over again.

Finally Buffalo hid himself in a large bush.
There he stayed quiet as quiet, and he
didn't bump anything. And the Wild Dogs
ran past, and they didn't see Buffalo at
all as he was so well hidden.

Buffalo didn't feel like bumping anymore. And he stayed quiet and still in the bush for a very long time.

Even today he stands motionless in the bushes and shadows,
where he knows he can't be seen because he hides so well.
And Bumping Buffalo no longer goes looking for trouble.

But if Buffalo thinks you are bringing trouble to him,
he will come charging out of nowhere...

...BUMPING
and
BUMPING
like anything!